In Memory of Jake

THE LEGEND OF JAKE, THE SALTY DOG

Written By Robert Gossett
Illustrated By Mark Yarbrough

John earned his living as a fisherman.

Jake shared John's love for the sea.

Early one Friday morning, John powered up their 36-foot fishing vessel and headed for the deep blue sea.

A dolphin jumped so high that he was flying.

A chorus of sea gulls sang their praises to a beautiful day.

Suddenly, the sky began to darken and the wind whipped to 60 knots.

Then out of nowhere, the Salty Dog was slammed by a 20-foot rogue wave.

Jake dug his paws into the deck and tried to fend off the storm with his mightiest growl.

But it was too late... the next 20-footer engulfed the small craft.

John began to lose hope as he watched their boat sink to the bottom of the Atlantic Ocean, but...

Jake refused to give up.
He paddled hard and headed
in a westerly direction.

... and three nights with John holding fast to his collar.

... he had paddled all the way back to South Beach.

Jake had *saved* their lives!

JAKE, THE SALTY DOG

HERO

Jake's place in nautical history is assured.

Glossary

Vessel — A big boat.

Knot — The speed of a boat. One knot equals one nautical mile per hour.

Nautical — Relating to the ocean, boats and sailors.

Rogue Wave — A large ocean wave – bigger than the other waves.

Engulfed — To swallow up.

Raging Sea — A powerful storm of wind & waves.

Instinctively — Natural, unlearned urge to do something.